ADRIFT

An Odd Couple of Polar Bears

Jessica Olien

BALZER + BRAY
An Imprint of HarperCollins Publishers

Karl and Hazel are not friends.

Karl thinks Hazel is mean.
She never wants to play with
the other polar bears.

She doesn't talk very much.
She likes to sit and daydream in a
quiet spot by the water.

Hazel isn't mean. She is just shy.

Hazel thinks Karl is too loud
and that he smells like old fish.
Which he does, a little.

One night there is a big

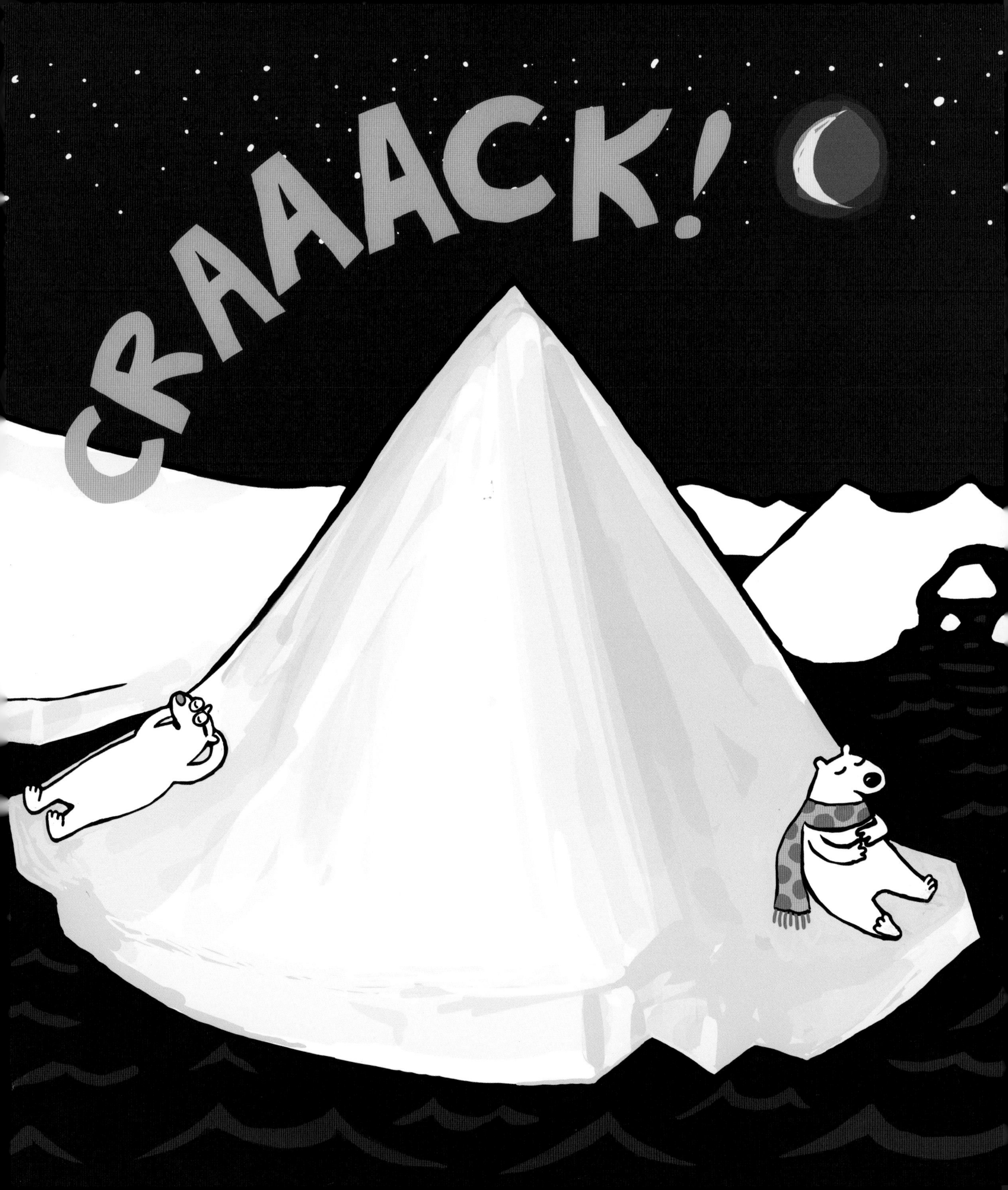
CRAAACK!

When they wake up, both Karl
and Hazel are alone.

In one direction, their home is getting farther and farther away.

In the other direction is an endless sea.

As they float south,
the ice floe melts,

and melts,

and melts.

Sigh.

!

Until . . .

Of all the polar bears, Karl is stuck with the one who doesn't like to talk.

Of all the polar bears, Hazel is stuck with the one who talks too much.

Then one morning . . .

After that, they get closer,

and closer.

After a while, Karl doesn't smell too much like old fish.
Or maybe Hazel has just gotten used to it.

Sometimes Hazel worries that the ice will all melt before they see land. But she doesn't tell Karl. She doesn't want him to be worried.

One morning, there is a tiny sliver of land on the horizon.

It gets bigger

They imagine what they will do when they get to this new place.

The land looks so big, bigger even than the ocean.
Suddenly they miss their little ice floe.

And they lived cozily ever after.

AUTHOR'S NOTE

There are many kinds of animals who are able to live in extreme cold and call the arctic home. Polar bears share their arctic habitat with wolves, walrus, seals, whales, narwhals, and puffins.

Polar bears weigh between nine hundred and a thousand pounds. That is more than you and ten of your friends combined!

Polar bears have webbed paws for swimming, and under their white fur they have black skin, which helps them absorb the warming rays of the sun.

The ice cap that covers the North Pole is shrinking, and only we can stop it!

If we don't, all the ice could melt and take away the homes of polar bears and other arctic animals.

Why?

Air pollution gets trapped inside the earth's atmosphere like the air inside of a balloon. This causes the earth to heat up and the ice to melt.

It is not only bad for polar bears but also for other animals, both on land and in the sea. It is dangerous for people as well, especially those of us who live near the ocean.

WHAT CAN YOU DO TO HELP SAVE POLAR BEARS AND PRESERVE THEIR ARCTIC HABITAT?

Find out what your local politicians are doing to prevent businesses from polluting. If they aren't helping, write them letters and emails asking them to get involved.

Unplug your toys and electronics when you aren't using them. Keeping things plugged in wastes precious energy.

Next time your family is about to hop in the car for a short trip, ask them if they'd like to walk instead. Cars are some of the worst pollutants.

Ask your friends and family to help you care for our beautiful planet!

LEARN MORE ABOUT POLAR BEARS:

http://kids.nationalgeographic.com/animals/polar-bear

http://gowild.wwf.org.uk/regions/polar-fact-files/the-arctic

www.sciencekids.co.nz/sciencefacts/earth/arctic.html

www.spri.cam.ac.uk/resources/kids/

To Pooky

Balzer + Bray is an imprint of HarperCollins Publishers.

Adrift: An Odd Couple of Polar Bears
Copyright © 2017 by Jessica Olien

Library of Congress Control Number: 2016935874
ISBN 978-0-06-245177-4

Typography by Aurora Parlagreco
16 17 18 19 20 SCP 10 9 8 7 6 5 4 3 2 1

First Edition